Aparna Vasisht

Playing Catch

Bumblebee
Books

BUMBLEBEE PAPERBACK EDITION
Copyright © Aparna Vasisht 2023
Illustrations by Nikhil Arora

A CIP catalogue record for this title is
available from the British Library.

ISBN: 978-1-83934-747-4

Bumblebee Books is an imprint of
Olympia Publishers.

First Published in 2023

Bumblebee Books
Tallis House
2 Tallis Street
London
EC4Y 0AB

Printed in Great Britain

Dedication

I dedicate this book to the wonderful community of Montclair,

who have shown me what it means when

we say "it takes a village" !

Rob threw the ball to Sia.

Neel sat on the bench. He wanted to play, but nobody ever picked him for their team. He was too slow.

He plodded toward Sia. "Can I play?" he asked.

Sia knew the teacher said they had to include everyone.

She handed the ball to Neel.

He threw the ball to Rob. Rob easily caught it.

It came flying back – Neel dropped it.

"Oh no!", said Sia, "let me have the ball".

Neel handed her the ball. "I didn't mean to drop it", he said looking downcast and went back to the bench. He felt really sad and his eyes filled with tears..

In class, Miss Trish asked him – have you been crying?

" Sia took the ball back. I wanted to play catch." he said.

Sia heard him and yelled back, "he dropped the ball—

he lost a point."

Miss Trish said it was time for their science class
but they would talk about it later.

They were learning about the body that day and as Ms. Trish pulled out the skeleton, it reminded Neel of his xrays. He had a great idea! He could show his xrays so his friends knew why he couldn't be faster.

The next day at circle time, Ms. Trish said,
"We have a special sharing from Neel today."

Everyone was very curious – they saw a large envelope lying on the floor in front of Neel.

Neel started –

"when I was born, I had curves in my spine

I have had 2 surgeries and
will keep having one every 6 months.

I go to the hospital and it hurts a lot for a few days.

My back has many screws to help me stand,

he said pointing to his Xray in the light.

It's really hard to run and I can bend only a little bit."

All quiet. Then one hand went up.

Yes Sia.

"So when we were playing ball, was it
hard for you to throw?"

"No, throwing was not hard. Catching is hard because I
can't run fast enough & I can't bend to catch"

"So we can be a catching and throwing team –
I catch and you throw!", Sia shot right back

"We can name it team-catch?"

A new game was born.

Neel beamed!
Finally, a game he could play with his friends!

About the Author

Aparna Vasisht is a long time resident of Montclair, NJ, USA; she lives there with her husband, two sons and two cats. In this book she shares a story that typifies an experience many children go through - both, children with disability and those without - the struggle for a child to fit in and understand another's experience and their openness to change once they do understand it! She is the mother of a child with a physical challenge and has learnt from him/with him as he has grown.

Acknowledgements

Thank you to my son, Eshaan, for being willing to share this story

CPSIA information can be obtained
at www.ICGtesting.com
Printed in the USA
BVHW061325280323
661280BV00007B/124

9 781839 347474